FOR ALL MY SOUTH AFRICAN FRIENDS, ESPECI
SAM, WHO INTRODUCED ME TO THE STORY.

— ALAN DUK...

FOR MY WONDERFUL WIFE, KEEGAN BLANKENAAR
AND PIET GROBLER – THIS BOOK WOULD BE
IMPOSSIBLE WITHOUT YOU.

— DALE BLANKENAAR

FOR THE PROTECTION AND CONSERVATION OF THE
ENDANGE D ANIMALS IN THIS BOOK.

— TINY OWL

Paperback edition first published in the UK in 2020 by
Tiny Owl Publishing, London

For thousands of years, people have been telling stories. From this rich global heritage, we can find stories that are strikingly similar but also different. *One Story, Many Voices* explores well-known stories from all over the world. For teacher resources and more information, visit www.tinyowl.co.uk

#QuillSoup

#OneStoryManyVoices



A catalogue record for this book is available from the British Library.

ISBN 978-1-910328-66-8

Printed in China

# QUILL SOUP

Alan Durant
Dale Blankenaar

Noko the porcupine was hungry and tired. He'd been travelling through the Valley of a Thousand Hills and hadn't eaten for days.

He saw a small village ahead and his spirits lifted. "Food and shelter at last," he thought.

Meanwhile in the village, the animals caught sight of Noko.
"There's a stranger coming!" squeaked Monkey.

"Quick, run to your homes!"
shouted Meerkat.

Noko trudged into the village.
It was silent and empty.

"Hello, friends!" he called.
But there was no reply.

Noko went to the first house
and tapped on the door.

"Yes?" said Warthog.

"I've travelled a long way and
I'm very hungry," said Noko.

"Do you have anything I can eat?"

Warthog shook her big head.

"I'm sorry," she replied. "I ate a
big lunch and all my food is gone."

65

Noko knocked at the next house.

"How can I help?" asked Rabbit.

"Please, I need some food," said Noko.

"So do I!" Rabbit exclaimed.
"My greedy brother came to visit
and ate all my food. I have nothing left."

Noko knocked at
Monkey's door.

"Yes, what is it?"
Monkey asked.

"I wonder if you have
any food to spare a
poor traveller?"
Noko inquired.

"We are *poor* villagers,"
Monkey grumbled.
"We don't have
any spare food."

So Noko went to
Aardvark's house...

and Meerkat's house...

and Pangolin's house.

But he came away hungry. None of them, they said, had any food.

By this time Noko was very tired and very hungry indeed. But his brain was as sharp as the quills on his back.

He could see from the villagers' sleek coats and rounded bellies that they were lying.

He knew they had food. But how was he going to get some?

He sat and thought, and after a while he came up with a plan.

"I wonder if I might have a little fire and a large pot of water," he asked the villagers.

"Of course," they replied.
They couldn't refuse him that.

Noko put the pot on the fire to boil.

"It seems I shall have to make my own food." He sighed. "I shall make quill soup."

He plucked three quills from his back and dropped them into the pot.

"But surely the quills are too hard and sharp to eat," Warthog said.

"Wait and see! Soon they will soften and release their flavour to make a delicious soup," Noko explained.

He bent over the pot and dipped in his paw.
Then he licked it and nodded.

"*Mmmm*, tasty," he said.
"Just how His Majesty likes it."

"You've met the king?" squeaked Meerkat.

"Many times," said Noko casually. "I always make him quill soup. He loves it."

Noko tasted the soup again.

“If only I had some carrots...” he said ruefully.

Rabbit's ears shot up. He wanted to taste quill soup that was fit for a king.

"I think my greedy brother may have left a carrot or two," he blurted and he hopped away to fetch them.

Noko added the carrots to the water and tasted the soup again.

"Lovely," he announced. "Of course, the king likes mealies in his quill soup..."

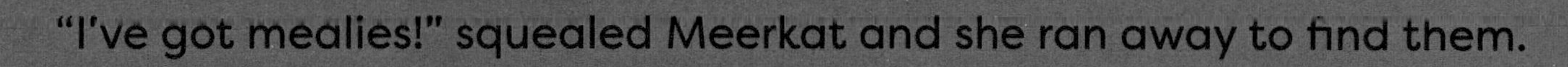

"I've got mealies!" squealed Meerkat and she ran away to find them.

Each time Noko tasted the soup, there was something that needed to be added: beans, peas, potatoes, spinach... In moments, as if by magic, all these things appeared.

Now Noko's soup was thick and rich.
Once again he tasted it.

"Perfect," he declared,
"unless... I don't suppose
anyone has a few worms?"

Pangolin did!

Noko told the villagers to fetch their bowls. "There's plenty of soup to share," he said.

And share they did! They drank bowl after bowl of the delicious soup in the firelight until the big pot was empty.

Noko sat back, looked up at the stars, and yawned.

"I wonder if you might have a hole where I could sleep?" he asked.

"A hole!" cried Monkey. "For our friend who has cooked delicious quill soup for the king?"

"And who has the generosity to share it with strangers?" piped Aardvark.

"No, my friend," said Monkey. "You, Noko, shall have the very best bed in my house."

"You're too kind," Noko smiled.

2067

Before they went to their beds, Noko and the villagers sang together, shared stories and danced in the moonlight.

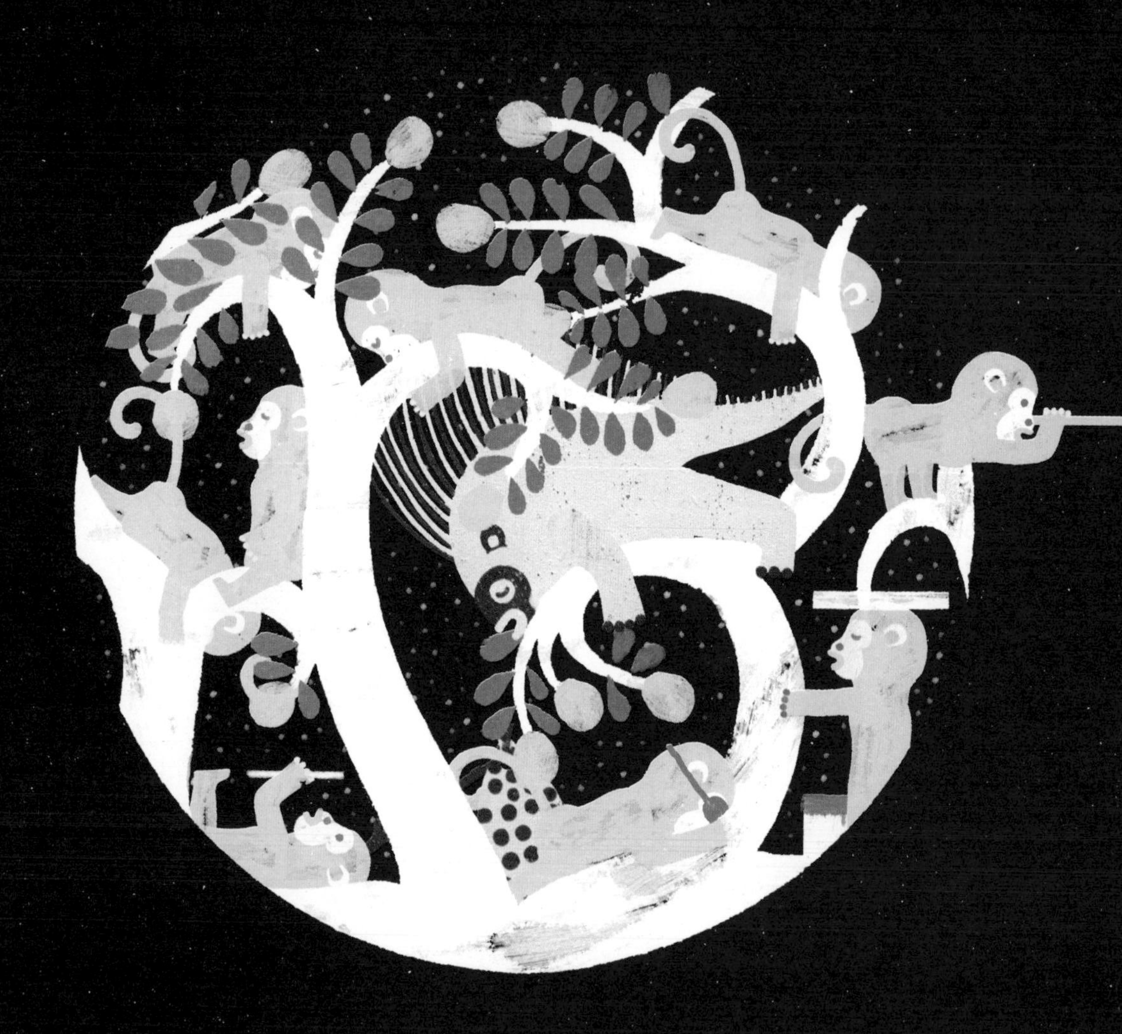

And later with a full tummy and a happy heart,
Noko the traveller went to sleep at last.